To ED:
FROM YOUR
COHORT (SUB)
HOSPITAL Jr

MW01608195

THE MAKING

OF

SNOW ANGEL

Joseph L. Pappalardo   12-2-12

The Making of Snow Angel
Copyright © 2010 by Joseph L. Pappalardo

All rights reserved. No part of this book may be reproduced or transmitted in any form or by any means without written permission from the author.

ISBN 978-0-615-39833-4

Printed in USA by: Publishers for Wordsmiths
                    35 Sierra Way
                    West Yarmouth, MA 02673-2622

Dedication

This book is dedicated to my devoted and loving wife Wilma for just being who she is and for keeping me on the righteous path of life. I could not have achieved all that I have, together with the many blessings from the Good Lord, without her generosity of spirit. She is truly my "designated" partner and friend. I love you back.

Introduction

This book was inspired by a variety of experiences that just seemed to coalesce into the story it has become. The first part of this puzzle began scores of years ago when I accidentally discovered the British metaphysician-philosopher, James Allen, whose writings in the early 20th century struck a nerve. This interest later led to a sabbatical odyssey to England to retrace his life and literature.

Later on when my first grandchild Cecelia arrived, I became charmed by her sweet innocence as we taught her how to make "angels in the snow" here in New England. This inadvertently became the second puzzle piece.

With the advent of the internet and electronic messaging, the accounts of children and their response to the meaning of love arrived in a hail of correspondence; which in turn, led me to ponder the meaning of love and life.

Now fully retired from college teaching, I had the luxury of time to let my imagination run freely on paper. Strangely, all of the items thus mentioned began to slide into place with characters and plots drawn together with a mixture of imagination, experience and whatever else. The story took on a shape of its own.

My own fascination with motion picture films somehow got thrown into the mix and so the Epilogue came into being as an integral extension of the original plot. In so doing, I found that I had unintentionally created a story within a story in a somewhat existentialist style. In telescoping these themes, I was able to truly re-examine the human experience by stepping outside of the main storyline.

It is my fondest hope that in sharing this personal exploration with the reader, he/she will be similarly inspired to re-examine the essence of our existence on planet earth. Thank you for your trust and understanding. JLP

Chapter 1

"Good morning children," said Ms. Souza, the school principal, in her very authoritative voice.

"Good morning Ms. Souza," replied the children with their usual Monday morning enthusiasm. They represented different age and grade levels for this special assembly.

"Today we have a special guest visiting us whom I told you about last week. Do you remember? It is Ms. Nancy Talbot from the local television station. She is here to talk to you about being on her program. I am sure you will recognize her from watching the five o'clock news channel every day. Did you know that Ms. Talbot and I were classmates years ago? We went to the same college as young students. Let me introduce her and she can tell you what she would like to do. Ms. Talbot."

"Good morning children. My, how bright and beautiful you look today! Before I begin, please call me Ms. Nancy, as I feel more comfortable when someone calls me by my first name. Now then, what I plan on doing is to ask you questions one by one, while Jim here gets you on camera. Then I will cut and paste the video at the station so that tomorrow night you may see yourselves on the news. Doesn't that sound exciting?"

With all the necessary explanations and answers out of the way, she went on to further explain that this was to be part of the station's Valentine's Day story. Students would be asked various questions about love and romance and they would offer their responses. Notices had been sent to parents earlier requesting permission to have children participate. The program would take on the format similar to the old Art Linkletter's, "Kids say the Darndest Things" show, and more recently updated by Bill Cosby.

As was to be expected, families of the children in the neighborhood school congregated in front of their TV's at home the next day, which was actually St. Valentine's Day. It was probably the most watched local news program in the area because of all the advance newspaper publicity. At approximately 5:15 p.m. that day, after most of the commercials had been aired, Nancy Talbot outlined her lead story to her public. Then she began her interview as the camera panned the kids. The following questions and answers were exchanged:

QUESTION: "HOW DO YOU DECIDE WHOM TO MARRY?"

KELLY, AGE 10: "YOU FLIP A NICKEL, AND HEADS MEANS YOU STAY WITH HIM AND TAILS MEANS YOU TRY THE NEXT ONE."

DAVID, AGE 11: "YOU GOT TO FIND SOMEBODY WHO LIKES THE SAME STUFF. LIKE IF YOU LIKE SPORTS, SHE SHOULD LIKE IT THAT YOU LIKE SPORTS, AND SHE SHOULD KEEP THE CHIPS AND DIP COMING."

ELAINE, AGE 11: "NO PERSON REALLY DECIDES

BEFORE THEY GROW UP WHO THEY'RE GOING TO MARRY. GOD DECIDES IT ALL THE WAY BEFORE YOU GET TO FIND OUT LATER WHO YOU ARE STUCK WITH."

QUESTION: "WHAT'S A GOOD AGE TO GET MARRIED?"

PAMELA, AGE 9: "TWENTY-THREE IS THE BEST AGE BECAUSE YOU KNOW THE PERSON FOREVER BY THEN!"

DOMENIC, AGE 7: "NO AGE IS GOOD TO GET MARRIED AT ... YOU GOT TO BE A FOOL TO GET MARRIED!"

QUESTION: "HOW CAN YOU TELL IF TWO PEOPLE ARE MARRIED?"

ERIK, AGE 6: "MARRIED PEOPLE USUALLY LOOK HAPPY TO TALK TO OTHER PEOPLE."

MICHAEL, AGE 7: "YOU MIGHT HAVE TO GUESS BASED ON WHETHER THEY SEEM TO BE YELLING AT THE SAME KIDS."

QUESTION: "WHAT DO YOU THINK YOUR MOM AND DAD AGREE UPON?"

NATALIE, AGE 9: "BOTH DON'T WANT MORE KIDS."

QUESTION: "WHAT DO MOST PEOPLE DO ON A DATE?"

ALEXIS, AGE 8: "DATES ARE FOR HAVING FUN, AND PEOPLE SHOULD USE THEM TO GET TO KNOW EACH OTHER. EVEN BOYS HAVE SOMETHING TO SAY IF YOU LISTEN LONG ENOUGH."

CARLOS, AGE 11: "ON THE FIRST DATE, THEY JUST TELL EACH OTHER LIES, AND THAT USUALLY

GETS THEM INTERESTED ENOUGH TO GO FOR A
SECOND DATE."

QUESTION: "WHAT WOULD YOU DO ON A FIRST
DATE?"

ANTHONY, AGE 9: "I'D RUN HOME AND PLAY
DEAD. THE NEXT DAY I WOULD CALL ALL THE
NEWSPAPERS AND MAKE SURE THEY WROTE
ABOUT ME IN ALL THE DEAD COLUMNS."

QUESTION: "WHEN IS IT OKAY TO KISS
SOMEONE?"

SUSAN, AGE 7: "WHEN THEY'RE RICH!"

BURT, AGE 10: "THE LAW SAYS YOU HAVE TO BE
EIGHTEEN, SO I WOULDN'T WANT TO MESS WITH
THAT."

MORRIS, AGE 8: "THE RULE GOES LIKE THIS: IF
YOU KISS SOMEONE, THEN YOU SHOULD MARRY

THEM AND HAVE KIDS WITH THEM ... IT'S THE RIGHT THING TO DO."

QUESTION: "IS IT BETTER TO BE SINGLE OR MARRIED?"

MATTHEW, AGE 8: "I DON'T KNOW WHICH IS BETTER, BUT I'LL TELL YOU ONE THING: I'M NEVER GOING TO HAVE SEX WITH MY WIFE. I DON'T WANT TO BE ALL GROSSED OUT!"

CECELIA, AGE 7: "IT'S BETTER FOR GIRLS TO BE SINGLE BUT NOT FOR BOYS. BOYS NEED SOMEBODY TO CLEAN UP AFTER THEM!"

PATTY, AGE 10: "SINGLE IS BETTER ... FOR THE SIMPLE REASON THAT I WOULDN'T WANT TO CHANGE NO DIAPERS ... OF COURSE, IF I DID GET MARRIED, I'D FIGURE SOMETHING OUT. I'D JUST PHONE MY MOTHER AND HAVE HER COME OVER FOR SOME COFFEE AND DIAPER-CHANGING."

QUESTION: "WHAT ADVICE DO YOU HAVE FOR THOSE ABOUT TO BE MARRIED?"

JOHN, AGE, 11: "THE FIRST THING I'D SAY TO THEM IS: LISTEN UP, YOUNGINS ... I GOT SOMETHING TO SAY TO YOU. WHY IN THE HECK DO YOU WANNA GET MARRIED ANYWAY?"

QUESTION: "WHAT DO A MAN AND A WOMAN PROMISE WHEN THEY GET MARRIED?"

HARLEY, AGE 9: "A MAN AND A WOMAN PROMISE TO GO THROUGH SICKNESS AND ILLNESS AND DISEASES TOGETHER."

QUESTION: "WHAT WOULD YOU SUGGEST TO MAKE A MARRIAGE WORK?"

TIM, AGE 8: "TELL YOUR WIFE THAT SHE LOOKS PRETTY EVEN IF SHE LOOKS LIKE A TRUCK!"

MARTA, AGE 9: "IF YOU WANT TO LAST WITH

YOUR MAN, YOU SHOULD WEAR A LOT OF SEXY
CLOTHES ... ESPECIALLY UNDERWEAR THAT IS
RED AND MAYBE HAS A FEW DIAMONDS ON IT."

QUESTION: "WHAT ABOUT GETTING MARRIED
FOR A SECOND TIME?"

JULIE: "MOST MEN ARE BRAINLESS, SO YOU
MIGHT HAVE TO TRY MORE THAN ONE TO FIND A
LIVE ONE."

QUESTION: "WOULD THE WORLD BE DIFFERENT
IF PEOPLE DIDN'T GET MARRIED?"

CURTIS, AGE 11: "THERE SURE WOULD BE A LOT
OF KIDS TO EXPLAIN, WOULDN'T THERE?"

LIZZIE, AGE 9: "YOU CAN BE SURE OF ONE THING
- THE BOYS WOULD COME CHASING AFTER US
JUST THE SAME AS THEY DO NOW!"[1]

The program ended with Nancy Talbot making a few glib comments about children and their very honest perspective. The show was a huge success generally speaking, except that one viewer in particular was not amused at all this "cuteness" coming from sweet innocence.

Chapter 2

The neighborhood school mirrored the close-knit character of the Prescott community. The student population of Adams Elementary hovered at 550 young souls. Grades K-4 together with a corresponding number of classes made for conservative student-teacher ratios. Ideally, it could easily be stated that every child throughout the school was known on a first name basis. Furthermore, each child came with a family history as well; usually for the better. The environment was warm and friendly in spite of the fact that this was an elitist college town.

Ironically, the college continued to enjoy a hometown flavor and attracted many of the locals due to economic and geographic accessibility. This atmosphere was nurtured by the institution's founding charter; i. e. a percentage of admissions was reserved for residents fueled by scholarships endowed by wealthy donors. This rather unusual philosophy perhaps reflected the humble origins of these benefactors. This phenomenon contrasted sharply with the prevailing trend of students migrating to distant colleges and universities. The small private college was affordable as a result and was sometimes jokingly referred to as a "glorified high school." Nonetheless, this enabled a significant number to attend college at a reasonable cost while retaining life-long friendships. Thus, few people moved and a sense of community emerged stronger still.

It was not so unusual when the guidance counselor invited the principal to discuss a "gut feeling" she had about a particular student. Alicia Souza was taken aback when Yoshi approached her with Natalie Paxton as the topic of conversation. Loading a video tape into the VCR, the two proceeded to view the Valentine's Day television program that was telecast several days ago. Counselor Yoshi Akura was careful to point out her observations to the principal;

namely, Natalie's verbal response as well as body language which she claimed might be cause for concern. That in itself was not alarming, but other accompanying behaviors were enough to make this an issue. The child was a known quantity having been at the school through kindergarten and now half way through 2nd grade. She was a bright student and one who thoroughly enjoyed her teachers and the company of her friends. She was not only socially adept but an excellent reader. After all, she was the daughter of Professor Jon Paxton and his wife Roz. In addition, Natalie always appeared to be well dressed and nourished. Her mother, who had been trained as a nurse and was now a hospital administrator, attended to all the things that came within the province of her daughter's well-being.

Mrs. Akura continued that Natalie was now beginning to distance herself from her teachers, friends and studies. It would appear that she was losing interest in most events which once filled her life with joy as she began to withdraw day by day. The opportunity to observe this on tape and replay it over again provided ample evidence for substantiation.

The principal was equally convinced that something had no doubt occurred to cause this change in behavior. It was with these facts that they agreed some form of action was necessary as soon as possible.

Chapter 3

A telephone call summoned Dr. and Mrs. Paxton to the school in short order. When they presented themselves before the principal and counselor, they appeared visibly less confident than compared with their usual professional demeanor. Above all, they truly loved their daughter Natalie most dearly.

The tape was played primarily for their benefit and then they were asked to share their observations. The image of that girl on the TV screen was not the same as the little girl they knew at home. However they were quick to point out that she may have been shy. Then Ms. Souza and Mrs. Akura provided anecdotal records for their perusal. Both parents were thoroughly shaken as they read through first-hand accounts that little Natalie was lately being perceived with personality changes. When asked to compare this portrait with her behavior at home, both parents displayed a more uncomfortable posture. They began with excuses ranging from Natalie not having fully recovered from a recurring and most recent asthmatic attack to their being absent from home due to professional demands. The father deferred to his research and the mother equally pointed to mandatory attendance at out of town conferences. Reluctantly and ashamedly they confessed to being inattentive to the developing situation at home. They were unanimous in declaring their affection for the child and how they would remedy the situation.

Yet, in spite of all their assurances, Mrs. Akura was not thoroughly convinced. She sensed a consistent theme in the parents' defensive maneuvering. As a guidance counselor for some twenty years, even in the safe and secure environment of Prescott, she detected a note of domestic dishonesty. Though united in their love of child and resolve to fix things, each offered a strategy that excluded the other parent. There was no mention of the "we" in any of their solutions. It would appear that father and mother were going their separate ways, though each pledged to help the child. Mrs. Akura wondered to herself how much like a thing to be owned a child must invariably feel; that is, in not being directly approached to share problems and more especially with regard to their resolution. She ended the day with the entire scenario playing over and over again in her mind, much like the video tape of the Valentine's Day program. She knew too, how she made all the right suggestions, follow-up procedures and the like and yet in her heart she was even more troubled after she opened up this Pandora's Box. How was this all to end … and what would become of her little student …?

Chapter 4

Rather than involve Natalie, the parents directed the counselor to, " ... wait this thing out and see what will happen ..." In such matters, who is to say what is right or wrong?

Surely, it is a judgment call with a 50-50 chance of it going in either direction. As it turned out, the child would learn of her parents' school visit in any event. A class mate had so informed her, so she was already aware that she was the center of concern and yet was not included to play an active role. The end result made her more guarded and insular. She began to withdraw from her studies and friends ever so slightly from day to day. Her real comfort came by withdrawing to her bedroom and confiding only to "Boo," her pet beagle. The bond between the two was intensified because coincidentally they shared the same birth date. Boo was the wizened and impartial listener perhaps due to his advanced age as reckoned in dog years.

Nonetheless, it provided Natalie with an opportunity to vent in open monologue fashion which she obviously needed. Sharp behavioral changes were not all that evident and so her parents simply regarded this as a stage in growing up. Whenever Roz and Jon discussed Natalie's behavior, the matter was either placed on hold or they minimized any significance. Thus, Natalie began to backslide emotionally and it was starting to surface at school. Against its collective judgment, but fearing to be labeled alarmists, the administration continued to play the waiting game as instructed.

Chapter 5

It began as an impromptu tag football game between classes at State University but ended in the infirmary as a scoreless tie. The forward pass Jon caught was actually not in the end-zone but on the hood of a parked auto. So intent on the task at hand, he failed to realize he was out of bounds. He awoke in the infirmary, ball still firmly in his grasp. He opened his eyes gazing at a goddess dressed in white. He thought he had died and gone to heaven. This angel of mercy was dabbing an anti-septic on his lacerated cheek. No doubt it would require a couple of stitches, she thought. This goddess spoke to him in gibberish so it seemed, but slowly he began to distinguish a word or two. Then he heard himself asking for her name. It was love at first sight for him although the student-intern was not at all certain if her patient was slightly deranged.

After being rejected by Roz several times on the telephone, Jon and his roommates hatched a plan. They would "borrow" a stretcher from the dormitory and rush him into the infirmary once again. Only this time he would be dripping with "blood." The cafeteria, in this case, was the donor of ample packages of ketchup. The plan would have succeeded except for a couple of comedic errors. At the time Jon was carried in, the ER physician who was a member of the teaching faculty was momentarily covering for an absent nurse-intern. It was purely coincidental but Roz had just stepped out to assist in a blood-donor drive. There was no backing out when the diabolical buddies discovered this change of events. That the doctor went ballistic at the severity of this prank mildly understates the situation. Just then, Roz popped back into the ER and exploded into laughter when the jig was unveiled. Jon lay sheepishly with the stretcher on the floor smeared with blood-red ketchup looking quite forlorn - and all alone as his mischievous mates had scattered to the winds. From that point on, the courtship began in earnest. The couple began keeping company regularly and were married at the end of the semester - his junior year - her sophomore year - a mere four months later.

For the next year the couple lived a fantastically romantic existence but occasionally faced economic hardship. This was not unlike other married couples at the time, as a mutual state of commiseration dwelled among them. After Jon received his bachelor's degree summa cum laude at State, they knew they could no longer postpone the decision confronting them. Would Roz be able to finish her studies and if so, how were they to survive?

Chapter 6

Nonetheless, Roz continued towards her nursing degree while fate had intervened for Jon. He accepted a doctoral teaching fellowship that enabled the young couple to remain on campus during her last year. They were not to remain a couple for long however, as they discovered that they were soon to be joined with child. The news was met with mixed emotions. Birth control measures were not working, or so it would appear. Evidently the young mother of twenty-two was constantly over-scheduled and somewhat lax on taking her contraceptive pills regularly. She attributed this to fatigue and demands of her academic program. Jon was less than enthusiastic. He had hoped that they might delay starting a family until completion of his graduate degree. By now he had made up his mind to pursue a teaching career in higher education. Recognizing the limitations that accompany a scholar's life, he had hoped to be somewhat established before having children.

Privately, and on occasion, he often questioned the desire and more especially his ability to be a father. Needless to say, the following months were filled with much anxiety for the partners. One was in awe of motherhood with all the attendant aches and pains. The other was more reluctant now about fatherhood, perhaps fueled by intense graduate study and research. Their problems were greatly compounded with limited income and ever-increasing expenses. Roz was the major bread-winner who was paid only for actual working days; and, the number of non-paid sick days was adding up. In most households, this pregnancy would be received with much joy but in this case several issues were beginning to become abundantly clear. Stress came in the form of complications during Roz's pregnancy. For one thing, the loss of income and the mounting prescriptions placed a major dent in their budget. On the other hand, they accepted the realization that the honeymoon was over with intimacy becoming increasingly infrequent. Reacting to these pressures the young couple conversed less often, occasionally snapping at one another. This tableau served as a prelude of things to come long after the baby arrived. Apparently selfish interests intensified, driving them further and further apart. Social obligations were becoming painfully awkward. Each had to call upon acting skills neither knew they possessed. These two basically sincere individuals came to feel as though they were living a lie. Slowly and privately, each one speculated whether family life would really work. Would the presence of a baby maintain the status quo; miraculously cure the relationship; or, in fact totally destroy the marriage? Ultimately, taking the noble road for the baby's sake as well as for appearances, they would behave in a civilized fashion. That is to say, they would peacefully co-exist under the same roof. At least for the present time. The baby arrived during the final year of Jon's residency.

Thanks to good health and fortuitously the small inheritance from Roz's old maid aunt, Jon made it to his Ph.D. in English literature. It had not been an easy year with Roz working shifts and Jon caring for little Natalie. He was literally juggling the infant on one knee, preparing meals and studying for his orals all at the same time with little or no sleep. Many times later on in life, he would marvel at how so much was accomplished. He attributed this to youthful energy and exuberance.

Surprisingly, the first job offer was the best one which Jon and Roz agreed upon and accepted. And that is how they came to Dickens College at Prescott. Their nestling into a domestic lifestyle was buoyed by the many social affairs held at the local hospital where Roz was now employed and at Dickens. The community also was alive with socio-cultural offerings providing the couple with a more or less neutral zone. In time they made accommodations and adjustments to their marriage as most couples do.

Chapter 7

Thirty-five Adams Avenue in Prescott exemplified the architecture of a picturesque New England Town. The houses were mostly colonial. It was rumored that U.S. President John Quincy Adams visited this very neighborhood; hence, the name given to the street. In town it was an enviable address to claim. Roz was extremely delighted that this should be their first home. That this was their good fortune necessitated even greater cooperation between the two. She bubbled with enthusiasm to refurbish and decorate in a tireless manner.

Baby Natalie's room was painted in a warm pink shade. The ceiling rained animated mobiles of favorite cartoon animals in every shape and color imaginable. It was in every respect, airy, bright and the ideal room for a baby girl. In fact, it was a room easily adaptable for a growing girl. An area carpet designed in an alphabet motif sat on the center of the wood parquet floor. All the bedroom furniture was painted soft white and sported animal caricature handles. The room was even spacious enough to accommodate a younger sister if ever the need arose.

To say that Roz was ecstatic at such a house would be a mild exaggeration. It was her opportunity to transform this domicile into a real home she thought. They had come into their own at last after having traveled down the road of low-cost university housing. Perhaps this is what the marriage needed besides having a child to care for, she added. Of all the rooms, she particularly freaked out about the kitchen. For it was here that she would not only prepare and serve the family meals but she would be able to supply the added ingredient of love. More and more, she came to believe that life was good and they had only come to a bump in the road. She envisioned a time when Natalie would fully capture her husband's heart. And to a certain extent, she would be right. However, it was not to happen quickly.

The idea of having his own private study thrilled Jon no end. He thought of the many long hours he would spend there preparing for class, reading papers and researching for eventual publication. The study was situated to one side of the living room and had a full view on both ends of tree lined Adams Avenue from the bay window. There were two entrances-exits, one leading to and from the front circular drive and the other to the mud-room and out the side of the house. It was entirely out of the way in terms of house traffic and would afford him the opportunity to come and go virtually at will. Truly, it was a private place for one to contemplate, write and confer with colleagues.

Chapter 8

Maybe it was because of the ill health her widowed mother and then her aunt suffered that motivated Roz into wanting to become a nurse. It was almost bound to be that way from the beginning. Some would even call it, "predestined." The three women lived together since her father died at a young age. It was then that her spinster aunt (being the bossier, older sister) decided she would move in. Economically she argued, it only made sense to pull together but they were really the only close family that was left. Roz was about nine years old at the time and maybe it was for the best the way things worked out. So depressed at her husband's death was the mother that she not only didn't oppose her sister's will but become increasingly sickly. It was as if she had lost the desire to live.

Only her love for her child and outbursts with her sister gave her occasional bouts of strength. By the time she was 43, her will and her heart gave out completely. Though only 14 now, Roz had become her most proficient and loving care-giver. For the next several years and even into college she similarly fulfilled the same role for her aunt until she too passed away. Roz was a compassionate young woman who dearly loved her mother, and though sometimes at odds with her aunt, came to know and respect her for her strength. The older woman played an important role in assisting with Roz's career decision. It was she who encouraged her niece to go into nursing. Besides, she pledged to assist with college tuition and having no family of her own, would provide a modest estate. Though any demonstrative signs of affection between them were practically nil, there prevailed a mutual understanding. And so it was that the red-haired teenager with smiling hazel eyes sparkled with wonder when first she entered State University.

There she would find her love and her life as wife, mother and nurse. Though she fiercely loved Jon, she sometimes feared that he would eventually learn how he became a father prematurely. She never confided in anyone and so she kept those thoughts to herself. She alone held the lock and more importantly, the key.

Professionally, Roz was a cracker-jack nurse. She was as tough as nails when the chips were down and as a gentle as a dove when the situation demanded. She had a perfect sense of proportion and control. Like her husband, she too graduated from State summa cum laude but this fact was not nearly as recognized as Jon's accomplishments. She lived in the shadows but was a superior supporting character unlike her husband. Hers was a giving nature and his was ego-centric. Though it was difficult to imagine for those who knew her, she was perfectly at ease with Emergency Room duty. She preferred this to other assignments, probably because of her internship at State which was open to this kind of duty. Though not as intense, this level of activity whetted her appetite for the challenge

of the unexpected. This strange turn of events may have
been prompted by her so-so humdrum family life. In a very
quick succession of events at the hospital, Roz was required
to do shifts and in no time at all, created a new position for
herself. So adept was she in the ER that she automatically
took to breaking in new ER personnel. This did not go
totally unnoticed by administration and she was ultimately
asked to write a job description for herself as Director of
Education for Nurse Personnel. She was to envisage a
broad scope of responsibilities that ranged from liaison
with State for recruitment of nurses, placement, in-service
program development and even as liaison with the local
school department for the short-term education of young
patients. Surely this was a feather in the nurse's cap and
one that gave her prestige and flexibility in her work
schedule. Having a young child at home made this
flexibility more desirable. Roz managed to accomplish all
this progress in a short three-year time frame. Just in time

for Natalie to enter kindergarten. It was really great timing. It also didn't appear as if another child was in the future. In a sense, she resigned herself to her status at the hospital as well as at home.

Chapter 9

As an Army brat growing up, Jon had moved extensively and now had no desire to travel. It would seem that he would instinctively nestle-in as it were without so much as a second thought. His dad was on the move just about every three or four years. Life was simply packing and unpacking from the time he was born. His two older brothers finding themselves without roots except for military-styled living, opted to follow Dad into the Army. In many ways Jon was the maverick. He was the junior and yet the first to break family tradition. He was not as mechanically inclined as his siblings growing up, preferring instead to read voraciously. In a manner of speaking, his heart was at home in this domain. He was immediately drawn to literature in both the visual and literary sense. As a toddler he became fixated on illustrations in almost any book at any age level. Then came the magical leap from pictures to sequential words. His curiosity grew as the search for truth and knowledge intensified. At graduate school he was torn between a love for literature and philosophy taking courses in both departments.

His skill at political maneuvering and negotiating matched his academic abilities he discovered at Dickens. Despite his youthful years, he was singularly granted rank of associate professor in two departments. The English Department would be home base while the Philosophy Department would be more in line with that of a visiting scholar. It established a precedent at Dickens predicated by his outstanding academic credentials and references. This unique combination was duly observed by many (with a degree of professional envy) but never replicated on campus. Additionally, Jon was given near total reign over course assignments and scheduling which was not difficult for him to accept. Needless to say, he did indeed feel that he was home - for the first time in his life. He felt he could at last shake the dust from his shoes and put down roots.

On the domestic front, he abdicated near total authority to Roz with the unspoken caveat that his study was his alone. Either pride, regret, ambition or any combination thereof may have been the compelling reason why he was professor primarily, husband next and then father in that order. In retrospect, he sought learning as the highest calling. Marriage was simply there as a convenience. Fatherhood on the other hand, was simply a responsibility he accepted as a consequence of his actions. Romance had transferred from the physical realm to the platonic, whereas in learning he subconsciously reasoned, the chase never ends.

The discretion to schedule his courses and times was liberating to say the least but it was only the tip of the iceberg in academia. For with these pluses were some minuses.

Jon began to find himself stretched with regard to other campus activities and responsibilities. Though this was primarily a private undergraduate college, the pressure to publish or perish still hung over his head. Admittedly, some of this pressure was imagined more so than he knew early on, if he were to earn promotion or tenure to full professor. Also, he wanted to push himself by leaving a back door open. Research and publications were necessary too, if ever he felt the need to move on or move up. Ultimately, he chose to play the game of devoting more time to research than he did to teaching. In truth though, he was always well prepared for class and his courses were usually over-subscribed with students. He was often sought out by the more serious-minded students who desired an education instead of just a degree. This was a credit to his reputation across the campus. Though usually regarded as a loner, he was friendly to all faculty and students alike and was considered an approachable professor.

In the same three year period that Roz made her mark at the hospital, Jon was able to achieve rank as full professor.

Serving diligently on the many campus committees earned him the admiration of his colleagues in a profession where professional jealously was ever present. Often times he felt over-scheduled to the point of distraction in conducting research. Eventually his research became an addiction in much the same way as a self-inflicted malady. It was to consume him and nearly lead to his own self-destruction.

Chapter 10

When they arrived at their new home that first August, Natalie was a delicate and yet playful toddler. She could have been a clone to her mother when she was that age. Her "terrible two's" were not going to be easy on her parents; or stated more precisely, not easy on her mother. For in truth, Roz was as the saying goes, "…chief cook and bottle-washer…" Jon by contrast, was too self-absorbed to be bothered with the mundane. Surprisingly, Jon's entire family was smitten with Natalie who more than made up for her father's apparent disinterest. They managed to accomplish a rapport while being in diverse areas of the country. Cards, toys, gifts and telephone calls frequently made their way to the household of the only niece and grandchild in the family. Mother and daughter were as close as any mother and child could be but as for Jon he remained somewhat detached. Occasionally one could detect a sense of brooding that approached mere tolerance of the child's existence. At times when he had no choice but to mind the child, she felt his uneasiness and fussed all the more. Roz attempted to arrange her work schedule so that she was literally the baby's sole caretaker; a skill she learned all too well growing up herself. She even arranged to run errands around Natalie's nap time so as not to inconvenience her husband.

Natalie was learning to assert herself as she progressed through the terrible two's. In some ways it looked as though she was mimicking her dad with his own negativism.

Being the natural charmer she was meant to be, the little girl ever so slowly began winning her father over. In turn, for some inexplicable reason, he heaped even more disdain upon Roz. Though he never raised the question himself, one had to ask if this behavior was rooted in pride, regret or whatever. Deeply, he originally blamed Roz for an untimely pregnancy and one that imposed some limitations and financial hardships. The continuing burdens of the latter were a constant reminder of this development. Nonetheless, Natalie was a joy to behold as everyone would attest. She drew rave notices everywhere they went. Each parent singularly rejoiced in this adulation in spite of the veil that stood between them. Natalie drew people toward her, and she did not hesitate to draw herself nearer to them as she ran from pillar to post. Then she further enraptured her admirers with that impish lisp that gave rise to the sweetest little voice. In every way she was a darling little girl.

Being the precious child that she was, Natalie displayed great interest in family photographs when she was about three and a half. On a particular wintry Sunday afternoon and feeling somewhat snow-bound, Roz decided to sift and sort through the pile of accumulated family pictures. Asking over and over again as children that age normally do, the youngster demanded to know who everyone was and what they were doing. Her interest was especially piqued when she saw photos of her mom as a little girl about her own age playing in the snow. It would be her introduction to snow angels. Of course she needed to find out what angels were in the first place. Though her mother treated the subject of angels delicately yet lightly, the child appeared puzzled to learn of the separation of life here and now and the life hereafter. Once the child mentally processed this reality as best she could, she wanted to know how one would go about making a snow angel. And could just anyone make one? Could she, she asked aloud? Being that kind of a day and with the storm now having abated, she begged for a real demonstration out-doors. Her mother could not resist her daughter's charm and the temptation to play at being a little child again. She thought of the privilege yet dual challenge of being both teacher and playmate all at the same time. Truly, this was a once in a lifetime opportunity that any mother would relish.

At first Natalie believed her mother to be taken ill, when Roz quick as a wink fell over backwards into the snow. Laughingly she invited Natalie to do the same and so she did as her mother asked. Then they played, "Simon Says" as both mother and daughter flailed their arms and legs from side to side as they lay in the fresh snow. When they arose and stepped back, they were able to see their perfectly imprinted angels in the white fluffy stuff. Afternoon shadows so accentuated the images that they were driven to take pictures of memories they created that day. From then on, it became an annual ritual between the two; particularly so on the first significant snowfall of every season. To ward off the chill afterwards, they sipped cups of hot chocolate topped with mint flavoring as a ceremonial conclusion to a day of frolicking. This event would become solidly entrenched as a family tradition which was to be shared with her father when cajoled on occasion. They would all look back over the years by way of their scrapbook from that point onward.

Chapter 11

Ever since the impending arrival of Natalie, the marriage began to flounder. To the casual observer, it might appear that no one was at fault, and yet, everyone was at fault; everyone except Natalie of course.

Roz and Jon in a sense were living lives apart, yet residing civilly in the same household. Natalie at 5 was now in kindergarten and enrolled also in a reliable neighborhood child-care program on the half-day. This enabled both parents to pursue their respective careers. Conferences, workshops and various speaking engagements placed each parent in great demand professionally. Some of this popularity spilled over into the community at large, necessitating social interaction with many other professionals as well. Occasionally they would be required to reciprocate in hosting social get-togethers. Theirs was a hectic schedule to say the least, each personally observing necessary protocols on the rise up the ladder of success.

In the privacy of the bedroom, theirs proved to be a rather odd arrangement. Though they were not openly affectionate toward one another, simply stroking the back of a partner's neck served to signal the need for an encounter. This usually occurred during the middle of the night without any foreplay or tender words exchanged. In this manner their needs were met about once a month. It was simply regarded as an answer to urge and/or duty and each held to his/her end of this silent arrangement. Until now there had been no evidence of infidelity.

Inevitably, scheduling conflicts in their professional lives surfaced, but this was to be expected. They were most gracious accommodating one another's commitments and usually worked something out. The area of most concern naturally had to do with Natalie. The girl was easy to please as she was shuttled from school to childcare and vice-versa. Or else, she would be minded by Mrs. Belfiore, the neighbor across the street, when gaps needed to be filled.

On occasion, she would even sleep over which was considered both a treat for Natalie and the senior Belfiore's. They came to regard her as they would a granddaughter. Roz considered her career as a vital part of her life but not nearly as much as when it came to being a mother. When resolving a family scheduling problem, it was usually she who would give in. After all, it was reasoned, Jon was the head of the household and so it was decided in this fashion. On one occasion, he found it necessary to attend a particular conference in New York on an area of growing interest to him. Steadily he was forging a stronger link between his love of literature and philosophy. As he grew older and more mature, the interest to explore more about philosophy began to surface. The conference entitled, "The Significance of Linguistics in Philosophy," intrigued him no end. He saw this as an opportunity to further his understanding of the association between the two disciplines. The only problem was that Roz would have to renege on an invitation to be a featured guest speaker at State's Department of Nursing. A great recruiting opportunity for her hospital would also be lost however, for the best candidates in the Honor Society were being inducted at the function. Tensions ran high between the two and for a while the situation appeared insoluble. It was then that Jon dropped a hint that his trip was also about furthering his ambitions. Prior to this revelation, husband and wife had exchanged harsh words that touched upon the underlying problem of his selfishness. Once again she capitulated.

The prevailing mood on the American campus scene was to develop a more inter-disciplinary approach. His own background and interests put him further along than he had originally intended. Now there was an opportunity for him to propose and possibly head a new Department of Inter-Disciplinary Studies. Naturally the two areas of English Literature and Philosophy would mark a prestigious beginning into the foray for Dickens. They had cleverly chosen the right person for this particular curriculum innovation unknowingly some years earlier. This would be a big pay-off for the college and for Dr. Jon Paxton, Professor of English and Philosophy. All that remained was for him to signal his intent to attend the conference as a presenter.

The skirmish revealed a sharper division between the two and a sign of events yet to unfold. Roz stayed at home as well might have been predicted. Jon left to deliver his treatise.

His original research had led him to the works of James Allen an early 20th century English philosopher-metaphysician.[2] So alive and imaginative was his presentation that it proved instrumental in earning a research grant to study abroad. Of course Dickens was more than accommodating in releasing him in light of this favorable publicity.

The notion of the family going abroad for a half year really excited Roz, although she would have to disengage herself from many previous commitments. She imagined the three of them would be provided with an opportunity to solidify as a family unit. Much to her chagrin, their relocation to England would not support that assumption. Jon was encouraged and driven by the grant more than ever. His withdrawal from the family became more acute. Lapses of indifference surfaced when Natalie would thrust herself upon her father's knee and so he would relent for the moment. Actually his affections with the child swung true to the expression, "…out of sight out of mind…" as when he was engaged in diligent research and writing; it was as if he were not in the present moment. All else mattered less to him.

Jon's work that fall semester involved travel to London, Birmingham, Leicester and Devon patterning a pilgrimage of sorts to Allen's haunts. Roz and Natalie tagged along with Roz doing most of the grunt work providing travel and lodging preparations. This was then followed by making some provision for dining whether in or out. She began to feel a growing sense of alienation with her husband yet bonding more intensely with her daughter. Fortunately the vehicle that expedited this bonding came in the form of working with Natalie in her 2nd grade assignments. Naturally though, she felt isolated because they were strangers in a foreign land without friends, family and a real home. She was sustained in the knowledge that this inconvenience would be short-lived.

At Ilfracombe in Devon, a quaint village quay by the seaside, they literally walked in the footsteps of Allen. It was here that the young metaphysician called home for the last ten years of his life. He wrote most prolifically with twenty volumes to his credit among other publications before he died at the age of forty-eight. At times his devoted and beloved spouse, Lily, collaborated in writing some of his material when James was not able. Her collaborative efforts were particularly meaningful as it led to the final completion and publication of works in progress upon his death.

The Allen's lived modestly in harmony with one another and their daughter, [3] who died at the age of 13 probably due to an outbreak of influenza. Together the trio was nourished by nature and strong spiritual beliefs though James was not particularly outgoing and not a churchgoer like Lily. Jon's attraction to Allen lay in his bridge-like phraseology from literature to metaphysics. There was an almost immediate identification to Allen upon the chance reading of the following verse:

As you think, you travel; and as you love, you attract. You are today where your

thoughts have brought you; you will be tomorrow where your thoughts take you.

You cannot escape the result of your thoughts, but

you can endure and learn, can

accept and be glad. You will realize the vision (not
the idle wish), of your heart,

be it base or beautiful, or a mixture of both, for you
will always gravitate towards

that which you, secretly, most love. Into your hands
will be placed the exact

results of your thoughts; you will receive that which
you earn; no more, no less.

Whatever your present environment may be, you
will fall, remain or rise with your

thoughts, your vision, your ideal. You will become
as small as your controlling

desire; as great as your dominant aspiration.[4]

Though not solely dependent upon poetry as a medium in

bridging philosophy, it soon became apparent to Paxton

that Allen was using language and common day experience

to shape the mind of man. This was awe-inspiring to say

the least and confirmed in him the affinity between the two scholarly disciplines as having real value. That is, to comprehend the relationships between and among man, God, nature and the universe.

On a particularly fine sunny morning, the Paxton's with the urging of Natalie, decided to picnic. Jon thought this to be especially pragmatic as he had wanted to walk the cairn where Allen lived. It was here that this thinking man had exercised early each morning and gathered up his meditations toward inspired writing. After a hearty and enjoyable lunch, Jon went ahead on the cairn taking his notebook along. Roz stayed behind to clean up with Natalie jumping and romping about. Without so much as a warning, a slight mist accompanied with fog moved inland and began to thicken as often is the case in Ilfracombe. Much to Jon's surprise, Roz asked if Natalie had gone with him for she was nowhere in sight. Likewise, Jon thought the child to be with her mother. Frantically they searched the dangerous rock-lined beach without result. In the few ensuing minutes, which seemed like an eternity, the fog became denser still. Just when hope was beginning to fade, Natalie appeared out of the grayness.

"Where have you been?" barked her father.

Timidly the little girl replied, "We just went for a walk to see the ocean."

"We?" demanded the mother.

"Yes, my friend and me."

"But I don't see anyone else," both parents said in unison.

"Well she and I met as I was walking and we just kept on going," was her reply. "She was so much fun and showed me where she plays."

"Well where is she now?" Jon wanted to know.

"Oh, she said she had to go but she walked me back here first because I was lost." Finally relief registered with mother and father and they gave up the interrogations. They hurried on back to their lodging.

Chapter 12

Now that the Paxton's were home in Prescott, Jon submitted his manuscript to the printer while sliding back into teaching for spring classes. Roz was on the road recruiting and training nurses due to a shortage of personnel. Natalie was eager to be reunited with her third grade chums at Adams Elementary again. Generally speaking it was to be a productive year for each family member though not particularly eventful. It was mostly like doing make-up work for the time abroad.

Toward the end of Spring Jon was called in by the Academic Dean, Dr. Clare Hutchins. It seems she noted that his publication had caught the attention of international scholars representing both worlds of literature and philosophy respectively. There was mention of his possible nomination for the prestigious Holberg International Memorial Prize (HIMP).[5] Clearly, she speculated, such an award would also put Dickens College on the global map, so to speak. Such a distinguished campus scholar might even be a prime candidate for her soon-to-be vacated post when she assumed the vice-presidency. Dean Hutchins, though a liberal feminist, was obviously quite proud of her role in acquiring Dr. Paxton's services initially. Though she warned that congratulations were premature, she was nonetheless delighted and thought a toast as a well-wisher was in order. Together they drank a cordial. With words of mutual respect and support, their meeting was adjourned. They were to keep one another appraised of any news relative to HIMP.

A curious thought occurred to Jon some days after his conference with "Clare" as she now preferred to be addressed. As excited as he was about the possible nomination, he reflected on the warmer side of his colleague. Though mostly career-driven, she had been previously married and now divorced for a little over a year. In that time she threw herself into her work at

Dickens. Jon detected a deeply feminine side in her demeanor, though he suspected a sense of loneliness. She was an extremely attractive woman in her late thirties or early forties, and surely he thought, would not have any difficulty in attracting a man if she were so inclined. The thought of what she said and how she said it, ran through his mind more frequently.

In the meanwhile, family life with Roz was cordial and at times even playful with Natalie or "Gnat," as he sometimes teased. She would insist that her given name was "Natalie." As always, they presented a proper family picture but there was a deeper, moodier side to the husband-wife relationship. Naturally this was never publicly displayed as they cautiously exercised reserve at all times.

The more Jon spoke of his increasing appointments with Dean Hutchins, the more Roz became jealous. This was the first time she ever felt this way about another woman simply because it had never been an issue before. But the jealousy was not directly aimed at Dean Hutchins as it was more a case of feeling hurt and betrayed. They had an arrangement she thought and she had held up to her part of their non-verbal agreement. Still there was nothing positive to indicate or even hint at infidelity.

The news obscured the centennial commencement at Dickens College. The public announcement coincided with the revelation of Dr. Jon Paxton's address as featured speaker and that he had been selected for the distinguished Holberg International Memorial Prize. The award was based on his on-going research and grant on James Allen which culminated in publication. Further, that upon the beginning of the next academic year in September, he would be returning as the new Academic Dean.

Over the summer and into fall, the closer working relationship between Hutchins and Paxton became more intense in many ways. Clare Hutchins similarly fantasized about her junior colleague as their professional rapport had begun to transform onto a more personal level. No longer obliged to teach classes, Jon found himself laboring longer throughout that summer and consequently drawn closer to Clare. What had in all earnestness started as preparation for the next academic year, she viewed as an opportunity to "cozy-up" to Jon.

"It couldn't just be my imagination" thought Roz to herself," but you would think now that its summer, we would have more family time." But that was not to be the case. As it turned out, she found that scheduling activities for Natalie and herself became more difficult. For while she worked a full schedule, and the "Gnat" was not in school, she still needed care. At the tender age of eight, she was full of vim and vigor and so Mom found herself engaged as her personal social secretary. The two of them worked to learn of available community activities. It was simply understood that whatever they planned would have to be without Dad. That's just the way it was. So it began with a week or two at camp for this or that, or swimming lessons, or the local recreational program or else a stay at the Belfiore's across the street. Jon rarely entered the picture except to respond to an emergency call from his wife when she was absolutely unable to either deposit or pick-up Natalie. It soon dawned on Roz that Jon's new position was just another millstone weighing down their marriage.

In truth, Jon too, found himself working longer each and every day. Though the nature of his work was increasingly administrative, he nonetheless found it fascinating. Fascinating, he mused, because he was able to make things happen for his teaching colleagues. He was after all, a teacher first and an administrator coincidentally. It was not difficult to see that he was to be esteemed by his peers to an even higher degree because he did not forget his roots.

What he apparently did not recognize was that he was neglecting his family. Although he enjoyed the status and responsibility as Academic Dean, that position did not necessarily grant him unlimited authority. Recalling his childhood as an "Army brat," he conceded to the old "chain of command" philosophy. This meant of course, that he would run new programs, proposals, courses, etc. through his immediate superior which in this case, happened to be Vice-President, Clare Hutchins.

His attention to detail and duty underscored his outstanding traits for scholarship. These were the very same qualities that she first identified when she originally hired Professor Paxton. This not only strengthened her faith in him but it also served to give affirmation in her own ability to attract talent for Dickens College. Perhaps she particularly delighted in the closer working rapport that was fast developing between the two.

Being summer, regular office routine was not that closely

observed. Some of the "conferences" between Clare and Jon were conducted at off-campus sites. Not all of these locations were at local eateries as neither was big on food or drink. That is not to say that they didn't occasionally have a drink or two. Sometimes, just to get a breath of fresh air, they would drive out to the nearby lake and discuss matters. It was on one such occasion that they accidentally ran into Roz retrieving their child from swimming lessons. The meeting was awkward to say the least, mother and child looked mildly surprised at seeing the other two. And while the conference was innocent enough, they stumbled upon their own words and made off in hasty retreat for the college. This left mother and daughter somewhat puzzled but Roz had the good sense to diffuse the incident by introducing a diversionary topic for conversation.

Then there were other times that Jon faced crisis situations that demanded Clare's input at the earliest possible moment. Matters ranging from budget requests, federal grant proposals, the hiring of new faculty, etc. left Jon with little time to act singularly. As urgent as the incidents appeared, he found it necessary to contact Clare at all times of day or night.

As summer pressed on and the school year loomed closer, Jon sought her counsel even more after hours. He thought he was beginning to get the "feel" for his new position as each day wore on. Then just before Labor Day weekend, Roz approached him about some "get-away" time for the family. After all she reasoned, "We haven't had a real vacation this summer and it would be good for us to be together with Gnat." For all his eloquence, Jon was at first speechless and then began stammering. All that Roz heard was one weak excuse after another for his not being able to go. That's when the proverbial shit hit the fan. Finally, after all the years of putting up with Jon and deferring to his career, Roz hit him with a barrage of accusations just between the eyes. "Where have you been all summer Jon? In fact, where have you been when I needed you before? Never mind that, where have you been for our beautiful daughter Natalie? Never mind, go back to that college and your new girl-friend. You would rather be there anyway. Isn't that your real home Jon? All you want out of our marriage is someone to keep your house, your kid and your clothes and make like we're the typical all-American family isn't it? Well go to hell MR. ACADEMIC DEAN! You can just stuff it like all your stodgy colleagues. You all deserve one another. Well it is all yours now Jon as I am leaving." Exit one Roz, wife and mother.

For one week Jon's calls to the hospital where Roz worked were refused. It was unlike him to plead for mercy but that is essentially what he did by leaving messages on her private voice mail. He felt as if he was advocating for Natalie but he actually was advocating for himself. Though he was stung, it was more a question of ego. In fact, he was downright pissed off because of Roz's poor timing in his estimation. The opening week of college classes is no time for an Academic Dean to play housemaid to a young girl. He was terribly inconvenienced and he didn't like it one bit. Though he never showed Nat any hostility, he felt uncomfortable using pretense to ask for the Belfiore's help. Generally speaking, his telephone messages to Roz went something like this; "Roz, please come home for Natalie's sake. There will be no questions asked until you are ready to discuss matters. Natalie misses you very much. I'm sorry if I hurt you." Of course, there was a slight edge to his voice as he labored over this oft-rehearsed speech. Roz detected this immediately. On the weekend, Roz reappeared as she would normally do after attending conferences. And that is how things were left for the moment. Family routine resumed as usual for the most part, with husband and wife acting civilly toward one another. They gave the best performances of their lives for their child's sake. And just as home life was "restored," Jon, who was quite unrepentant, continued in his work unchanged and unfettered. That is, he worked long and hard, day and night either closeted with much reading or else in one conference or another. Those sessions, particularly with Clare, appeared to be increasing. His behavior was back on track and later on both Roz and he would broach the subject of his relationship with his boss. In a sense, this was regrettable for it was pushing him further away and closer to Clare. Their discussions also began to touch lightly upon the early years of their marriage and their struggle with educational expenses and the demands of parenthood. So Jon sought Clare for emotional support more and academic counsel as subterfuge. Eventually their relationship became less and less discreet. They would not hesitate to dine at popular restaurants and be seen enjoying themselves in public throughout the semester term.

To make matters worse, Jon was invited to accept his Holberg Prize in Copenhagen in early December shortly after Thanksgiving Day. Because of the international notoriety, the board of trustees approved a measure to send Vice-President Hutchins to represent the college. The hidden agenda in all of this was that she viewed this as prime opportunity not only to seize stolen moments with Jon but to gain some notoriety for herself professionally.

In Copenhagen there was much fanfare to be had what with endless series of parties preceding the awards ceremony, tours and speech-making, etc. It was a dream come true for Jon. Free from all responsibility, he felt all the more intoxicated and liberated with this new-found freedom. He and Clare spent a glorious week of sheer romantic delight slipping then plunging into ecstatic love-making. It was difficult for either one to have imagined that this week would end soon; but even further, how this relationship would continue back in the States.

Roz had literally been left in the dark even while Jon was planning his trip abroad; for no mention of anyone accompanying Jon had ever arisen. The only topics discussed about family not being in attendance were Natalie's problematic asthma kicking up again, as well as school and travel concerns. It was not until the Prescott Journal ran a front page picture of Jon accepting his award that Roz spotted Clare standing by his side. This really raised her dander as Jon, who never had never openly lied to her or was ever unfaithful to this point, was caught red-handed in an act of omission; or, worse yet!

Much as they tried to be discreet with their talks at home, husband and wife were in deep difficulty now and those late evening talks were becoming heated. It was not surprising that Natalie could sense something was wrong with voices rising often times. On one such evening, the youngster was aroused from her slumber as their voices echoed to her upstairs bedroom.

In very subdued tones at first, Natalie heard her mother accuse her father. "Jon, you have betrayed us," she went on to say. Although Natalie didn't understand exactly what was going on, she sat on the staircase trembling in fright as she detected something in her mother's voice.

"You deliberately lied to us about your trip to Copenhagen by not telling us you were not going alone. I had to read about it in the newspaper and be humiliated before the entire community. Bad enough rumors of your indiscretion were circulating about beforehand. This now provided ample evidence to all the townsfolk. Do you think we are all stupid while you live in that ivory tower of yours?"

Jon's only defense and a poor one at that, was his silence on the issue. He stood alone, shame-faced, indicted and found guilty as charged.

Then rising to dig himself deeper in a hole, he charged Roz

with, "Have you ever thought about why I would go with another woman? Why I have had to struggle so hard to overcome the mistakes of our youth?" Roz looking puzzled entreated, "And what mistakes did we make?" her voice rising and quavering. "You know quite well what I am talking about," he responded. Clearly she did not, although the direction of the debate was making her more uncomfortable. Jon countered, "Well the baby for one thing." "What? … About, Natalie?" she demanded in escalated tones. At the sound of her name, Natalie at once knew she was now at the center of this argument. "Well, you knew that I was not particularly keen on the idea of having children, but I at least conceded to wait until we could best afford one or two." Hearing this, the child on the staircase gasped for breath as she realized that she was unwanted by at least one parent, her father. Though he was not an affectionate man, she always had the deepest respect for him. Fortunately the next words she heard mollified her somewhat. "You know how much I love our child, but we have paid a price of nearly ten years in playing catch-up with all our bills. This might have been prevented if only you could have waited to have a baby Roz." He continued to plod on ever further, "I have long suspected that you lied to me about taking your birth control pills regularly which could have bought us a little bit more time. Isn't that true? Or, will you continue to lie to me for another ten years?" Her worst fear confirmed, Roz realized that Jon knew all along that she was not totally honest. While she was sorry for that and what it may have done to their marriage, she was not going to apologize for having brought a new life into this world.

The two of them remained quiet for the next five minutes staring at their coffee cups on the kitchen table. Then true to form, she stood to clean up before retiring, he turned to go into his study, and Natalie unnoticed, scrambled to her bedroom; sobbing under the covers with her arms wrapped around Boo until she fell asleep.

Chapter 13

Getting through the Christmas Holiday was difficult. Now everyone had become an actor, pretending to skirt the issue eating away at the family. Even Natalie bravely put on a happy face. Underneath her façade however was a bewildered child. She was not exactly certain whether what she heard was only a dream or the real thing. Also, she was not clear about some of the words her parents used. She especially had trouble accepting the notion of being unwanted while at the same time receiving the loving attention her parents gave her. She concluded she might be the cause of all those late evening outbursts she overheard as they became more spontaneous and more intense.

It was at this time that she started losing interest at school. Her teacher, Ms. Knoss dismissed this at first, thinking she was competing with the focus on Christmas or perhaps that Natalie's asthma was coming on. In any event, she gave the child some space.

The only redeeming feature about family life was playing outdoors with Mom. And January was right around the corner and with it, the promise of snow. Frolicking outside and having snow ball fights, making snowmen and especially making snow angels were her delight. She would ask her mother about her childhood and those family photos of when she was first introduced to making snow angels. Roz would never tire of recounting the same stories over and over again. After nearly an hour of play time, it was necessary to culminate the activity by re-enacting the ceremonial serving of hot chocolate with a touch of mint flavoring. Natalie found the entire experience to be soothing and comforting enveloped in her mother's love. School was another matter however, as the New Year brought even more marked behavioral changes in the child. Her teacher, acknowledging that the excitement of Christmas had passed, was relieved most children were now re-focusing on their studies. All except for Natalie, who once removed from her mother's love, could feel all alone even in a group of children. Further, Ms. Knoss also perceived that the girl was becoming insularly detached from the other students. A pre-occupation with self, thought the young mentor. She would attempt to approach Natalie on a one-to-one to get her to talk but found her to be quite guarded. What she was not able to witness, were the ever-increasing discussions between the parents that only heightened Natalie's frustration. After all, who does a young child turn to if not her parents? Even though she may feel as though she was the cause of some family disharmony? How could she even broach such a hurtful topic? So the inner tension she felt intensified as time went on. Finally, Ms. Knoss sent an anecdotal report to the guidance counselor. Eventually other school personnel would similarly submit such reports to guidance.

Chapter 14

Nearly a month elapsed since the TV broadcast of the Valentine's Day program. Still no definitive action had been taken to curb Natalie's attitude. School personnel were taking a wait and see approach while her parents were overly invested in their own pursuits as usual.

An unsuspecting snowstorm was to change the normal course of events. The heavy snow totally caught the forecasters by surprise. So much so, that most schools and businesses were forced to close for the day. Finding themselves locked in so to speak, husband and wife took to squabbling early on that afternoon. Rather than to expose Natalie to acrimonious recriminations, Roz dispatched Natalie to the Belfiore's across the street. The child bundled herself up in her winter snow suit and boots and left with a heavy heart knowing full well what was to ensue. Outside, she would make a snowball and roll it in the heavy wet snow down the driveway. When she safely crossed the street, she thought about making snow angels in the deep blanket that had accumulated. She pretended to be playing with her usual playmate, her mother. Purposefully she let herself fall backward knowing the impact would be cushioned. Once down on her back, she began flailing her arms and legs from side to side occasionally rising to inspect her white on white art work. She had become very proficient in creating perfect snow angels. Enjoying all the privacy in the world on the far end of her neighbor's garage, Natalie decided to catch her breath by simply lying down with the cold, moist flakes hitting her face. This seemed to take her mind off family affairs for the moment though she felt terribly cold and more especially alone.

After an hour or so, Roz telephoned her neighbor to inquire about Natalie. When Mrs. B expressed surprise as to the child's whereabouts, Roz and Jon sprang into action. After a few fruitless searches, they eventually found little Gnat still lying down surrounded by beautifully shaped snow angels. She was wet and turning blue by this time. They reasoned she had experienced an asthma attack and was unable to get herself up. They were so alarmed at her condition, that they thought it best to head straight for the hospital.

Natalie's condition steadily deteriorated developing into pneumonia. The child lay in a coma and remained so until May. She expired peaceably without ever regaining consciousness on a warm and sunny day just before Memorial Day. Needless to say, her parents, neighbors and classmates as well as the entire community were stunned at so tragic a loss of a little life.

Chapter 15

Rubbing her eyes slowly, Natalie felt refreshed as she looked here and there for some familiar landmarks. In the background she could hear soft melodic strains of music being played. Everywhere she turned she saw dazzling white brilliance but it did not hurt her eyes. She felt her feet moving under her but really had no sense of where she was going. Compelled to continue, she began to hear her name sung in a chorus of low whispers which seemed to get louder and she quickened her pace in that direction. A hush befell the stark surroundings and then a woman in a heavenly voice announced her name. "Natalie, Natalie, Natalie. Welcome home little one."

The astounded girl cried out, "But this is not my home. I want to go to my own home with my mommy and daddy."

"This is your new home now," the spirit echoed back."

"This is where you came from in the very beginning and now it is time to return." Even more anxiously the "little one" rebutted, "I am not ready (hesitating) … to leave mommy and daddy." At this the spirit took on a human-like form with angelic characteristics to comfort her more. Still Natalie appealed, "Mommy and daddy will be very sad and I, too, will be very sad for them. You see, I don't think I ever made them happy. They quarreled a lot over me you know." "But that is not your fault child," echoed the apparition. "All parents argue at one time or another. That's just what happens." The haughty miss insisted, "Well, I'm simply not going with you until I make things better for them."

Acknowledging this great impasse, the spirit proclaimed, "Child, because you have so much love to give, you will be granted a short extension before making a final entry into God's holy mansion. Henceforth you shall be designated an "Angel in Waiting." And you shall also be given the help of a "Guiding Angel." With this the heavenly vision vanished and another appeared. "Natalie, it is so good to see you again." Wiping away a tear, Natalie looked up and saw her play mate, Genevieve Allen whom she befriended in England. This momentarily puzzled her then perked her up a bit and the two embraced for a long while.

Chapter 16

Jenna then assured little Natalie that the two were "kindred spirits." It was practically inevitable that their meeting during the Paxton's sabbatical to England was pre-ordained. That is, that Jenna had been dispatched as a premonition of events to yet unfold. Being several years older, she was deemed a worthy Guiding Angel.

Slowly, Gnat developed a trusting dependency with Jenna. While she was more accepting of her fate, she nonetheless continued to remain anxious about her parents' relationship; particularly more so now that they anguished over the loss of their only offspring.

Though nearly a century in real time actually separated the two girls, they discovered they had much in common. With Jenna taking the lead, they exchanged family stories and played games together. The older girl explained how she found peace in her new world and how eventually she was reunited with her mother and father. Further, that time in this new dimension was not measured as it is on earth and that their reunion actually appeared to occur in short order. This latter tidbit buoyed Natalie knowing that a similar meeting with her own family would not be that far off. Seemingly endless hours of conversation between the two transpired. They spoke of their first encounter, friends, school, and games and so on. The younger girl looked upon the other girl more like a big sister she never had and wished she had known her as she had existed on earth. Of course their favorite topic was talking about their respective families. Jenna speaking about her internationally famous dad and her very devoted mother. Despite her youth, Natalie grasped the similarity between the two sets of parents. The most conspicuous and outstanding coincidence eventually turned upon their early demise and their being an only child. This latter fact indeed cemented their bond and it was then that Natalie understood what it meant to be a kindred spirit with another being.

Chapter 17

The giddiness of young girls resounded gleefully in the still atmosphere. Throughout all this playfulness however, and as persistent as ever, the task at hand was not forgotten. Somehow, they would have to intervene in the lives of Natalie's parents who now chose to live apart. Bringing them together would not be that simple though Roz and Jon, in a sense, had lived separate and often lonely lives under the same roof. It was tantamount to peaceful co-existence up until now. The time for grieving was long and difficult for each one. In their solitude, self-reflection and grief were often inter-mixed with pangs of characteristic guilt.

Over and over again Roz asked herself how their estrangement came about and what affect it had upon Natalie. She sensed that in the end, she was not happy and personalized the dissatisfaction in a failing marriage by blaming herself. And throughout this period of inner turmoil, she also sought to blame her husband. She was especially upset with his selfish life style and aloofness toward the family in general and her in particular. He was in fact, the reluctant husband as well as the reluctant father, she thought. His commitment was half-hearted, offering no more than mere tokenism. His was a comfortable life of scholarly pursuit with built in house-keeping privileges. Yet in the furthest recesses of her mind, Roz felt a twinge of guilt herself for not being up front with Jon. Then again later, she would feel badly for not having asserted herself earlier in their marriage and confronting this issue.

Jon, on the other hand, experienced profound emotional mood swings. At times he felt thoroughly drained and his usual smug self-confidence was reduced to nil. His normal routine was in total upheaval with none of the usual creature comforts in place. He found himself pre-occupied with sorrow over the death of his daughter and the part he may have played in not being the total father. Perhaps he thought, he was directly responsible for her unhappiness and consequently her untimely passing. Maybe he also could have been more of a husband, he thought. If he ever felt anger, it was not directed at Roz but toward himself. He was so distraught that he was now under a doctor's care and taking medication to balance his moods. Furthermore, he was thinking that this would be the time to take a personal leave from the college. He would plan to return for the spring semester.

Natalie, with Jenna's direction, conceived an action plan whereby she would strongly influence her parents' thought waves. This would be accomplished through subconscious dream episodes and consciously through the power of suggestion with certain objects appearing most propitiously. Different scenarios were advantageously envisioned to occur under special circumstances. This would activate a mind-stream of related thoughts dealing with family life in happier times.

Chapter 18

The fourteenth of each month became especially painful for each parent as it was the anniversary date of Natalie's death. The first year was a double whammy for they had to deal with her burial and then Memorial Day fast approaching. It was not uncommon for Natalie to appear in their dreams or for them to imagine seeing her face upon every child in shopping malls and the like. Similarly, each was consumed with overwhelming emptiness for their beloved daughter. The stage was totally in sync with the plan concocted by the Angel in Waiting; i.e. for her to appear in their dreams on the eve of each month's anniversary date, or perhaps, for some nostalgic possession of Natalie's to strangely surface out of nowhere. This pattern of events was increasing in frequency throughout the summer and into the school year. Oddly enough, but simultaneous with the plan, her parents would visit her grave on holidays and each month on the anniversary date.

On coincidental encounters, one would patiently wait for the other to leave the site before paying respect. One time Roz came upon Jon sobbing uncontrollably and she was deeply saddened to see how much pain this man was suffering. She paused, allowing him to compose himself, before kneeling down alongside Jon. Prior to this meeting, they would occasionally exchange passing glances.

On this particular Thanksgiving Day, they smiled less awkwardly and eventually broke into discourse with one another. Each one expressed surprise for being there on this holiday. Behind reddened eyes they saw the hurt and the loneliness. Each one felt a sense of longing for a time since past. Roz actually felt pity for this once proud man who now appeared to be nothing more than a shell. She saw how much he realized that which he had lost and how humbled he had become. Natalie and Jenna thought their magic was working ever so subtly as they looked down upon this tableau.

Finally Roz penetrated the silence by half asking, "It would be a shame for each of us to be alone this first Christmas without our darling. Jon, would you like to come for dinner then?" This totally disarmed the man who no longer thought only of himself. He was embarrassed as he stumbled, "Why … I really hadn't thought about … But, why … yes … yes …that would be nice." He turned to leave and then holding back tears, stared directly into her eyes. After a while and barely audible he said, "Thank you Roz … thank you." One could see Roz was visibly shaken to see her husband so genuinely moved and so transformed. She instantly realized this feeling of compassion welling up inside of her was an indication of her undying love for him.

Chapter 19

Roz was filled with both anxiety and anticipation as she flew through the house making last minute preparations. Would Jon arrive as he had promised or was he merely being polite when he accepted her invitation? To ward off these ambivalent feelings, she thought to turn on the stereo for some cheery Christmas music. It had been six months since Natalie slipped away and it was time for them to move on. Jon would understand, she thought. The nagging concern rattling in her brain was that, " … Christmas wouldn't be Christmas without children …" How do parents ever get past that, she wondered? It never seems so permanent and final, but that was the only answer she came up with. She had to resign herself to that she felt; at least for the time being.

Being the orderly person he was, Jon respectfully rang the front door bell. He did not presume to just waltz in. "Strange," … he had thought to himself as he approached

… "this is my home and yet I feel like an outsider." The door opened and she greeted her husband with a nervous smile and a sweet kiss on his cheek whispering, "Merry Christmas to you Jon." His apprehensions evaporated and he breathed a sigh of relief. He was reminded of Roz's gentleness that first attracted him to her; first, as the most meaningful woman in his life and then as wonder-mother to his beloved and departed daughter. He pondered once more as he often did lately, about how wrapped up he had become with his work. How wasteful and how utterly foolish, he concluded.

His sense of smell appeared to be working overtime from the beginning. Roz's perfume reminded him of sweeter, more delicious times of their life together. The balsam fir, as always, made for the perfect Christmas setting particularly as it filled the living room with its distinct fragrance. Then last, but not least, the hot pork roast quickly activated his taste buds as he anticipated the first home cooked meal in a long while.

He had remembered to bring some great Italian pastry that the Belfiore's had introduced them to earlier. In addition to the dessert, he brought several gifts which he placed under the tree when he passed through to the dining room. One was labeled, "To my wife and dearest friend, Roz." Another one simply read, "Dearest Roz." The third contained the words, "To the best Mom - ever," signed, "Love, your daughter Natalie." Finally, the last gift was distinct because of its size and most colorful wrapping paper. It simply read, "To Gnat our most beloved child - Merry Christmas." Boo had torn open his chew toy unceremoniously and was already hard at work.

Jon was thankful the music played throughout the meal for there was not much conversation. The little that there was, pretty much focused on her work at the hospital. His free time, now that he was on leave, seemed to be spent doing more creative writing.

After the mid-day dinner, the two sat down by the tree to exchange and open presents. The usual pile of packages was now reduced to a relatively humble mound of items. Roz remembered how he was always losing gloves and so he was very pleased when he unwrapped the brown, lined, leather replacements. Knowing his wife and her sweet tooth, she was thrilled with his choice of Swiss chocolate miniatures; also, a gift certificate at her favorite specialty shop. The third gift, the one from Natalie was a snow globe from the same specialty shop that the two had once admired. At this, Roz raised it to her face and kissed it gently as a tear rolled down her cheek. Moved by the thoughtfulness of this careful selection, she then reached out her hand to Jon. Then they gazed at the last box labeled, "To Gnat." It was agreed that they would open it together. Jon's gift, now their gift to Natalie, was a Winnie-the-Pooh cuddly doll in which she had expressed an interest. The two just sat there on opposite ends of the sofa with Pooh in the center. Each visualized how excited their daughter would be snuggled with all of them there.

To while away the long desolate hours after the tragedy, Roz renewed her interest in painting. She took Jon into the rec room and unveiled her portrait of their child executed strictly from memory. It was a particularly poignant moment for the parents as it revealed how the artist saw the child in her mind's eye.

Later on, they would go to the cemetery and be joined again in spirit as a family. On their arrival, Boo, the lonely pet Beagle, instinctively headed toward the burial site. It was there that Jon carefully removed Pooh from its gift box and laid it upon the shelf of the headstone. Then Jon fell on his knees and broke down, sobbing uncontrollably.

Roz, looking down at the inconsolable man pitied him and asked him to return to the family homestead. From that moment forward, he was never to leave.

Chapter 20

Roz thought she would try to reconstruct the dream in her mind and then share it with Jon. As they headed downstairs she began by saying her dream was particularly disturbing. Natalie had appeared before her once more. She remembered having the courage to ask, "Is that really you Natalie or am I dreaming again?" "Yes mother, this is Natalie. I am okay here but I miss you and daddy very much. I have a friend here now and that makes me feel better when I get sad." Roz continues, "Natalie, can you give me a sign that this is really happening and that it is you I'm talking to; promise?" "Yes mommy I promise to send you a sign." Though it appeared there was more to this dream, Roz was content in recalling what she could. When they arrived at the kitchen table, Roz found a huge Valentine's Day card and a bouquet of flowers that Jon had thoughtfully placed there the evening before. She thanked him with a very romantic kiss. Just before she proceeded to prepare breakfast, she raised the window blinds behind the sink to look out at the new day. She was amazed to find a heavy blanket of fresh fallen snow that was not expected. She gasped for breath and could not speak. Alarmed, Jon sprung to his feet to provide assistance as she motioned for him to look out the window. And there it was as plain as day. In the middle of their back yard was the imprint of a perfect snow angel. The truly surprising thing was there were no footprints in sight - anywhere! Just when husband and wife realized this was Natalie's promised sign, a dazzling beam of light came down from the heavens transfixing itself on the snowy imprint. Then briefly they thought they saw their little one standing resplendent on this lighted pathway and then slowly disappearing as she ascended.

Unbeknownst to the parents, Jenna too appeared on this lighted path but was not visible to them once again. With an extended hand, she called out, "Your work is done

Natalie, now come and play. The others are waiting for us." Smiling and with their hands joined, they began their heavenly journey. Surprisingly, a wisp of a spirit brushed by earth bound and Natalie became enormously filled with emotion. Without a spoken word, this spirit communicated the following to her, "Hello sis, I'll take it from here. Your baby brother loves you and will finally get to meet you again in time." Amidst all this glorious splendor, a heavenly choir heralded the making of a snow angel.

Exhausted and in total shock, mother and father turned toward the table and prominently awaiting them were <u>three</u> steaming cups of the ceremonial hot chocolate; and oh yes, complete with a sprinkling of mint flavoring.

Epilogue

"Well," asked the younger man in addressing the older, bearded gentleman, "What do you think? Has it any merit as a film?" The questions were not readily acknowledged. Only prolonged silence followed. The young man, accustomed to this reaction, took it to mean that his questions were still under consideration. Ultimately, the father gesturing apologetically mumbled something like, " ... well that good old boy, Frank Capra, would have gone for it, I'm certain." Max was only too eager to please his dad in locating a workable script and follow in his footsteps as a film director. He stood transfixed by this response. What did his father mean by that? Did he or didn't he like the story-line? Still, the son wanting to press on thought it over and then finally hesitated. Instead, Igor continued, "There are so many dimensions to making a film and the thing to keep in mind is, the story alone does not necessarily make for box office. In fact, this theme manifests the predicament of countless couples and they will not pay to see their likenesses on the screen. Perhaps if it were well scripted and exceptionally cast, it could follow in the shadow of, 'It's a Wonderful Life.' With all the rating categories of today, a family oriented movie might just find its niche." The Zeller's, though separated by thirty years, fell silent and began to fast forward to the various possibilities that might translate into a hit. "Who knows …" each one thought to himself, " … maybe this too, could be the sleeper of the year in Hollywood." Walt Disney it's not, but then a walk to the bank is more than just a walk when one is smiling along the way. They kibitzed through the evening and even into the early morning hours. What child star would be cast as Natalie; or, for that matter, the moody Jon and the very compliant Roz? They imagined dozens of candidates for each role every time bowing to an individual's charisma and thus possibly succumbing to multiple and costly script changes.

Especially important were the inter-active chemistries of the actors and the crafting of the script. The mission therefore was to parallel Capra's magic in, 'Life,' and yet make it contemporary.

Max's vision was in sharp contrast to Igor's realism. The young idealist desperately wanted to make "the perfect picture," if ever such a possibility existed. The seasoned veteran on the other hand, was fully aware that few such dreams succeed.

For better or worse, they agreed to exercise an option for the script. These included making changes to the original story with or without the author's collaboration. Finally, while open to the author's casting suggestions, the father and son team would ultimately choose the players. Further, the duo decided to take the entire matter under advisement for a period of two weeks before proceeding further. At that juncture, they would exchange their separate concepts for a finished production. Each one was to critique the script at leisure and with restricted privacy of course. Lastly, at the end of the month, they would reconvene to hash and re-hash one another's point of view. The sole purpose of this time frame and technique was to become familiar with the plot, and main characters, etc. but also to remain open to other rewrites. The senior Zeller also required the time to seek out backers who might be willing to finance the film. Having been in the industry for nearly fifty years, he knew his way around. Of course, this was analogous to a double edged sword that cut both ways. For in that same period of his worldly expertise, many associates had died; the industry had been totally transformed; and the nature of venture capitalists was likewise not standing still.

Even before the month came to a close, Igor broke the pact with his son and called him over to the house. They needed to talk about the project. His manner and tone signaled trouble to Max. "It's not going to sell sonny boy. No use spending any more time and money on this dog. None of the new guys on the street are willing to put up the bucks. We might as well cut our losses and run away from it too." Maxie was disappointed but not surprised. Though chaffing at the bit to become heir apparent to his father's reputation, he respected the old man's view. Still, he had to ask, "What exactly was the problem? Were they afraid of costs? ... competition? What then?" Igor scratching his few wisps of silver hair responded, "Well, do you remember how we likened it to, 'It's a Wonderful Life'?" "Yes," agreed his son. "Ironically, trying to make the backers see it this way was in effect, the kiss of death. Some young punks either didn't recall the movie or offered to puke right there on the spot. All they can think of, is today's box office and how the only road to success is through either sex or violence or both. I guess I've become prehistoric and don't even realize it." Sensing the mood of the new generation, yet still valiantly defending his father's old world values, Max simply nodded apologetically. "I even suggested some big name actors for the draw. They only responded that the story-line was just too blah and couldn't stand up on its own. So you don't think there's really anything we can do then huh Pop? " "No I don't" came the swift assent. "The story doesn't have substance though it's long on sentimentality. A major rewrite would entail more time and money. Better to cut our losses as I said earlier. This story, though cute, just won't make it today, period, exclamation-point!"

The two, in synchronized fashion, scaled their copies of the untitled manuscript onto the huge teak and leather desk. Theirs was a gesture of resigned unanimity. Then each toasted the other with an evening cordial to conclude the funeral. They then strode out the room to shoot a relaxing game of pool. On the way out, Igor turned off the lights leaving the study darkened.

"Come on wake up, wake up for heaven's sake. Don't you realize what's going on here, arose a voice in the darkness. They are selling out like the rest of society." "What do you mean?" asked Roz of her husband. Then suddenly the story book characters became life-like again as if rising out from the world of their slumber. "Those so-called movie producers are saying that there is no meaning here; that our story is not worth telling. That it cannot stand on its own merit; and that what we did as parents and how Natalie lived and died need not be told." "Yes, I see," replied Roz, but there really is a message here and they don't seem interested in seeing it to the end." In their grief, they reached out to one another in a tender embrace.

For now, their fictitious lives nearly spent, they reflected upon the past and the opportunities wasted by real life couples. Their thoughts turned to their darling daughter whose character was extinguished by the mere mention of acute asthma. Though only story book personalities, the tragedy of their daughter dying at such a tender age was so very real and life like. They wondered how painful the sorrow must be for parents in the external world. Would other parents have been able to learn something from their tale if it ever made it to the silver screen, they questioned; knowing only too late of lost chances at happiness? Fame and fortune in pursuit of one's career provide no comfort at a time like this. Family must come first, Jon posited. It was at this point that as Roz and Jon tried to recall a fuzzy dream and the making of a snow angel, both characters slowly dissolved into the quietude.

THE END

Endnotes

[1] An adaptation from an anonymous internet posting; November 30, 1998.

[2] James Allen was an actual person; however, some accounts of his life have been fictionalized. Before he died at the age of forty-eight at the turn of the twentieth century, he produced twenty books along with other publications.

[3] Genevieve is believed to be the name of Allen's daughter; hence, the nickname, "Jenna."

[4] Abstracted from, "As A Man Thinketh." Allen, James. New York: Thomas Y. Crowell Co.; circa 1913, 4th edition, p. 42; (Original: London: Savoy Press, 1903). This book became an international best seller having been translated into 22 languages in his lifetime and still enjoys brisk sales.

[5] The Holberg International Memorial Prize (HIMP) is an actual and prestigious award; albeit, literary license has been exercised for this fictitious tale.

Publisher's Note

This is a work of fiction. Names, characters, places, and incidents are the product of the author's imagination or are used fictitiously, and any resemblance to actual persons, living or dead, business establishments, events, or locales is entirely coincidental.

Made in the USA
Charleston, SC
24 August 2014

32695130R00051